Date: 4/17/20

BR 428.62 MAR
Markovics, Pearl,
Snail to mail /

by Pearl Markovics

Consultant:
Beth Gambro
Reading Specialist
Yorkville, Illinois

Contents

BEARPORT
PUBLISHING

New York, New York

Snail to Mail

I see a
yellow **snail**.

3

I see a little **nail**.

I see a
green **pail**.

I see a wood **rail**.

9

I see a
furry **tail**.

I see a white **sail**.

I see lots of **mail.**

Important Information

PRESORTED
Standard
U.S. Postage
PAID

15

Key Words in the -ail Family

mail **nail** **pail** **rail**

sail **snail** **tail**

Other **-ail** Words: **flail, hail, jail, wail**

Index

About the Author

Pearl Markovics enjoys having fun with words. She especially likes witty wordplay.

Teaching Tips

Before Reading

✔ Introduce rhyming words and the **–ail** word family to readers.

✔ Guide readers on a "picture walk" through the text by asking them to name the things shown.

✔ Discuss book structure by showing children where text will appear consistently on pages. Highlight the supportive pattern of the book.

During Reading

✔ Encourage readers to "read with your finger" and point to each word as it is read. Stop periodically to ask children to point to a specific word in the text.

✔ Reading strategies: When encountering unknown words, prompt readers with encouraging cues such as:

- **Does that word look like a word you already know?**
- **Does it rhyme with another word you have already read?**

After Reading

✔ Write the key words on index cards.

- **Have readers match them to pictures in the book.**

✔ Ask readers to identify their favorite page in the book. Have them read that page aloud.

✔ Choose an **–ail** word. Ask children to pick a word that rhymes with it.

✔ Ask children to create their own rhymes using **–ail** words. Encourage them to use the same pattern found in the book.

Credits: Cover, © patpitchaya/Shutterstock, © givaga/Shutterstock, and © Oleksiy Mark/Shutterstock; 2–3, © Ivan Marjanovic/Shutterstock; 4–5, © jetaboon/Shutterstock; 6–7, © irin–k/Shutterstock; 8–9, © cunaplus/Shutterstock; 10–11, © zokru/iStock; 12–13, © De Visu/Shutterstock; 14–15, © Michael Burrell/iStock and © Quang Ho/Shutterstock; 16T (L to R), © Michael Burrell/iStock, © Quang Ho/Shutterstock, © jetaboon/ Shutterstock, © irin–k/Shutterstock, and © cunaplus/Shutterstock; 16B (L to R),© De Visu/Shutterstock, © Ivan Marjanovic/Shutterstock, and © zokru/iStock.

Publisher: Kenn Goin   **Senior Editor**: Joyce Tavolacci   **Creative Director**: Spencer Brinker

Library of Congress Cataloging-in-Publication Data: Names: Markovics, Pearl, author. | Gambro, Beth, consultant. Title: Snail to mail / by Pearl Markovics ; consultant: Beth Gambro, Reading Specialist, Yorkville, Illinois. Description: New York, New York : Bearport Publishing, [2020] | Series: Read and rhyme: Level 1 | Includes index. Identifiers: LCCN 2019007360 (print) | LCCN 2019012639 (ebook) | ISBN 9781642805932 (ebook) | ISBN 9781642805390 (library) | ISBN 9781642807080 (pbk.) Subjects: LCSH: Readers (Primary) Classification: LCC PE1119 (ebook) | LCC PE1119 .M28594 2020 (print) | DDC 428.6/2—dc23 LC record available at https://lccn.loc.gov/2019007360

10 9 8 7 6 5 4 3 2 1